THE BILLY GOATS GRUFF

Retold by Cecilia Egan

Illustrated by Vasili Chuck

Cover by Elizabeth Alger

FINGER PUPPET BOOKS

First published in UK in 1989 by
Random House UK Limited
30-32 Bedford Square
London WC1B 3SG

© Egan Publishing Pty Ltd. 1988
Australia

Printed in Australia

FOREWORD

This brilliant new series combining books and finger puppets are fun, and will encourage both reading and imaginative play. Children will enjoy playing the parts of their favourite characters. Their concentration will improve as they listen carefully to the story and act it out.

Children and parents can enjoy using these colourful and attractive puppets to stage their own finger puppet show. There are ten classic fairytales and nursery rhymes to collect.

The three Billy Goats Gruff lived in a meadow where the grass was dry and yellow, and not very tasty. There was Great Big Billy Goat Gruff, who was truly enormous. He had long, strong horns as big as elephants' tusks, and when he walked, the ground shook.

There was middle-sized Billy Goat Gruff, who was an ordinary goat with ordinary horns. When he walked, his hooves scattered pebbles.

And there was little Billy Goat Gruff, who was extremely small, with tiny horns not much bigger than your finger. He walked very lightly and carefully so as not to tread on beetles.

Now, the three Billy Goats Gruff were not getting very much enjoyment out of the dry yellow grass. Alongside their meadow there ran a deep and narrow gorge, and on the other side of this gorge was a mountain covered with tall, green, juicy, tasty grass and lots of pink and yellow flowers, and no beetles to step on.

There was a bridge over this gorge, and you may well ask why the three Billy Goats Gruff did not cross this bridge to go and live on the mountain where they could get fat on tasty grass. The answer is this; a nasty troll lived under the bridge, and he used to eat anyone who tried to cross over.

But one day, the three Billy Goats Gruff said to each other, "We're tired of this grass. Let's see if we can get across the bridge to the tasty-looking grass on the mountain."

So they thought of a plan.

Little Billy Goat Gruff was the first to cross the bridge. "Trip-trap, trip-trap," went his extremely small hooves on the bridge.

"Who's that trip-trapping over my bridge?" snarled the Troll.

"It's me, Little Billy Goat Gruff."

"I'm going to eat you up," snarled the Troll.

"Don't eat me up, I'm too small to make a good meal," said Little Billy Goat Gruff. "Wait for my brother — he's bigger."

"All right then, off you go," said the Troll.

"Trip-trap, trip-trap" went Little Billy Goat Gruff, safely over the bridge to the mountain.

Next came Middle-sized Billy Goat Gruff. "Trip-trap, trip-trap."

"Who's that trip-trapping over my bridge?" shouted the Troll.

"It's me, Middle-sized Billy Goat Gruff."

"I'm going to eat you up," shouted the Troll.

"Don't eat me up, I'm not big enough to make a good meal," said Middle-sized Billy Goat Gruff. "Wait for my bigger brother."

"All right," said the silly old Troll. "Be off with you."

"Trip-trap, trip-trap" went Middle-sized Billy Goat Gruff, safely over the bridge to the mountain.

Last of all came Great Big Billy Goat Gruff. "BOOM, BOOM, BOOM, BOOM." When he walked, the bridge shook.

"Who's that boom-booming over my bridge?" bellowed the Troll.

"It's me, Great Big Billy Goat Gruff."

"I'm going to eat you up," bellowed the Troll, who had already set the table ready for his meal.

"OH, NO YOU'RE NOT!" said Great Big Billy Goat Gruff, and he lifted that nasty Troll up on his huge horns and tossed him so high and so far that he was never seen again.

So the three Billy Goats Gruff all got safely across to the mountain, where they lived happily on juicy green grass and pink and yellow flowers. They frolicked all day and grew sleek and fat, and they never had to worry about beetles or trolls again.

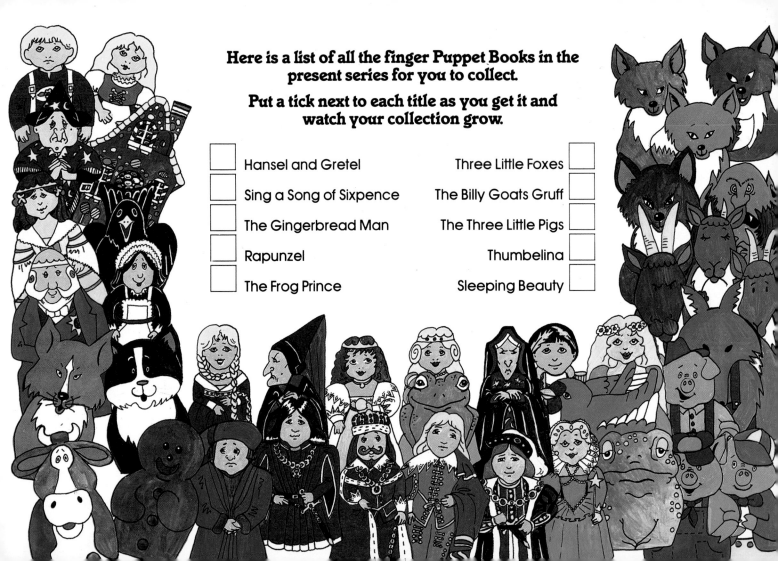

Here is a list of all the finger Puppet Books in the
present series for you to collect.

Put a tick next to each title as you get it and
watch your collection grow.

- [ ] Hansel and Gretel
- [ ] Sing a Song of Sixpence
- [ ] The Gingerbread Man
- [ ] Rapunzel
- [ ] The Frog Prince

- [ ] Three Little Foxes
- [ ] The Billy Goats Gruff
- [ ] The Three Little Pigs
- [ ] Thumbelina
- [ ] Sleeping Beauty